Buster Hits the Trail

by Marc Brown

LITTLE, BROWN AND COMPANY
New York ᕞ Boston

Little, Brown and Company, Time Warner Book Group
1271 Avenue of the Americas, New York, NY 10020 • www.lb-kids.com
First Edition
Library of Congress Cataloging-in-Publication Data
Brown, Marc Tolon.
Buster hits the trail / Marc Brown.—1st ed.   p. cm.—(Postcards from Buster)
Summary: Buster and his father visit South Dakota and send postcards home describing their visit to the
Crazy Horse monument, their experience with buffalo, and more.
ISBN 0-316-15900-X (hc)/ISBN 0-316-00121-X (pb)
I. Title. II. Series: Brown, Marc Tolon. Postcards from Buster. [1. South Dakota--Fiction. 2. Crazy Horse
Mountain (S.D.)—Fiction. 3. Bison--Fiction. 4. Postcards--Fiction. 5. Vacations--Fiction. 6. Rabbits—
Fiction.]PZ7.B81618Bje 2005 [E]--dc22   2004016165

Printed in the United States of America • 10 9 8 7 6 5 4 3 2 1

Page 3, 11 bottom, 35, 42: Photos by South Dakota Tourism. Other photos from *Postcards from Buster* courtesy of WGBH
Boston, and Cinar Productions, Inc., in association with Marc Brown Studios.

Do you know what these words MEAN?

buffalo: a huge animal with a big shaggy head and a hump on its back, also called a bison; buffalo live in North America

corral: an area with a fence around it that keeps animals from roaming

dogie (or dogey): a motherless calf

Lakota: a Native American tribe found in the western part of the U.S.

mosey: to stroll or saunter

prairie dog: an animal that is related to squirrels that lives in the western part of the United States

roundup: a gathering together of cattle in order to count, brand, or sell them

STATEtistics

South Dakota

- Mount Rushmore, in the Black Hills, is a memorial to four American presidents: Washington, Jefferson, Theodore Roosevelt, and Lincoln.

- The sixty-foot-high faces were carved between 1927 and 1941.

- Mount Rushmore is sometimes called "The Four Most Famous Guys in Rock."

"So, Buster," said Arthur,
"what will you be doing
in South Dakota?"

Buster put his hands on his hips.
"I'm going to mosey out
to look for little dogies," he said.

"What?" said Arthur.

"I'm just practicing my cowboy talk,"
Buster explained.

When Buster and his father
got to South Dakota,
they took a good look around.

"These sure are wide-open spaces,"
said Buster. "I'll bet the skies are not
cloudy all day."

"Do you want to see
Mount Rushmore?" asked his dad.
"Those four presidents
have pretty big heads."

Buster checked in a book
he was carrying.
"Dad, what about this, instead?"
he asked. "The biggest sculpture
in the world is right here.
It's called Crazy Horse."

Buster tried to imagine
what the sculpture would look like.

Dear Arthur,

How are things home on the range?

I have not seen the deer
or the antelope play yet.

But we haven't been here long, so
there's still plenty of time.

Buster

The Crazy Horse monument
was not what Buster expected.

Crazy Horse was a leader
of the Lakota Indian tribe.

"When Crazy Horse
was around horses,"
the guide explained,
"the horses would dance."

Dear Binky,

If someone made
a big statue
of you,
where would you
want to put it?

(Outside my
bedroom window
will not
be allowed.)

Buster

Binky Da
10 Pine Tree
Elwo

Only Crazy Horse's head
was easy to see.

"His nose is thirty-two feet long,"
said the guide.

"Wow!" said Buster.
"If he ever sneezes,
they'll feel it for miles around."

The rest of the sculpture
was not finished.
"It takes a long time
to carve a mountain,"
the guide explained.

Dear Brain,

I met a boy named Chris
and we visited the
Crazy Horse monument together.

He's a member
of the Lakota tribe.
He's LEELAWASHTE.
That means "cool" in Lakota.

Buster

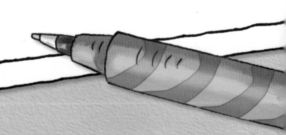

Alan Th...
22 Oak S...
Elwood...

Buster and Chris saw artists
working on the sculpture.
Some of the work involved blasting.

They watched from a safe place.
There was a big explosion
near the horse's eye.

"At Crazy Horse," said the guide, "we measure progress in tons and in decades. We have hundreds of thousands of tons to go yet. But it doesn't matter how long it takes—just so that progress never stops."

MODEL OF
FINAL SCULPTURE

2028

"Do you know why Crazy Horse is pointing?" asked the guide.
"He is pointing at the Black Hills. He's saying, 'My lands are where my dead lie buried.'"

"Crazy Horse must have been an amazing person," said Buster. "This place really makes me want to know more about him and the Lakota."

Dear Fern,

Since you like
to write poems,
maybe you'd like
to write one about
Crazy Horse.

Not many
words rhyme
with Lakota, so
be careful about that.

Buster

That night Buster was still excited.
"What else can we do here?"
he asked his father.

"Well," said Mr. Baxter, "we could go see
a buffalo roundup."

"That would be great!" said Buster.
"I've only seen buffalo on postcards."

Dear Francine,

Tomorrow, I am going to see some buffalo.

The Lakota people called them TATONKA.

The Lakota believed they were a sacred animal. You may have seen buffalo on old nickels. They're much bigger in real life.

Buster

Francine Frensky
Maple Drive
Elwood Cit

At the roundup,
Buster and his dad
met Bob and his grandson Levi.
Bob was an outfitter.
His job was to
show visitors around.

"So what is it like out there?"
Buster asked.

"Imagine you're chasing after buffalo
on a good horse," said Bob.
"You're cracking your whip,
and yelling, trying to get them
all going in one direction."

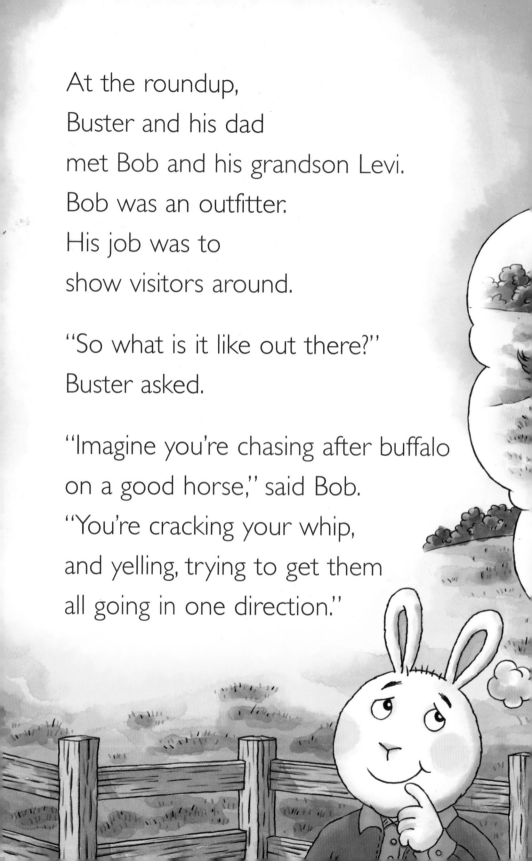

Dear Muffy,

I think being a cowboy is a lot harder than it looks.

But I know you would pick out the perfect saddle to ride on.

Buster

"Wow!" said Buster.
"But why can't the buffalo
just run free?"

"We need to take care of them,"
Bob explained.
"In two hundred years,
we want the herd to look
just as good as this one does now."

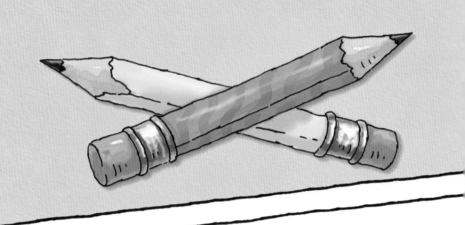

Dear D.W.,

I'm going to watch some buffalo get their yearly checkup.

They do get shots, but they don't have to open their mouths and say, "Ahhhhhh!"

Buster

D.W. Read
100 Main 9
Elwood Ci

When Buster walked up to his horse, he spoke very quietly. "Whoa . . . There's nothing to be scared about."

The horse snorted.

"I was talking to myself," Buster added.

Out on the trail,
Buster saw an antelope.
"So this is where they play," he said.
He also saw mountain goats
and prairie dogs.
But he saw no buffalo.

Dear D.W.,

Prairie dogs are not like regular dogs.

If you told Pal they were dogs, he would be confused.

Buster

"How will we know the buffalo when we see them?" asked Buster.

"Well," said Levi,
"the herd will look like
a big black-and-brown spot."

"What if we miss them?"
Buster asked. "I might blink
or something."

"There are 400 animals in
the herd," said Levi.
"You won't miss them."

Dear Arthur,

I did a lot of riding through the wide open spaces.

I could describe them by saying that they were very wide and very open.

Buster

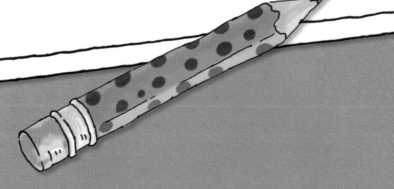

Suddenly, the buffalo appeared.
They came thundering down
from the ridge.

"Hey," said Buster.
"I thought cowboys only rode horses.
Some of these guys
are using pickup trucks!"

"Of course," said Levi.
"This is the 21st century, after all."

It took a while,
but finally all the buffalo
were herded into the corral.

At the campfire that night,
Buster thought about his day.
"Those *tatonka* were
really amazing, Dad.
They were worth waiting for.
But it feels mighty nice bunking down."

"So what will you dream about?"
his father asked.

Buster yawned. "I'm too tired to dream.
After a long day of hitting the trail,
I just want to hit the pillow.
Good night."

Dear Levi,

There are no buffalo in my neighborhood, but there are still interesting things to see. If you ever want to go biking on my trails back home, I hope you'll come for a visit.

Buster